First published in the United States, Great Britain, Canada, Australia, and New Zealand in 2010
by North-South Books Inc., an imprint of NordSüd Verlag AG, CH–8005 Zürich, Switzerland.
Distributed in the United States by North-South Books Inc., New York 10001.

Library of Congress Cataloging-in-Publication Data is available.
Printed in China by Toppan Leefung Packaging & Printing (Dongguan) Co., Ltd., Dongguan,
P.R.C., April 2010
ISBN: 978-0-7358-2315-0 (trade edition)
1 3 5 7 9 ⑨ 10 8 6 4 2

www.northsouth.com

JK-3
LaN

I WON'T Comb My Hair!

By **Annette Langen**
Illustrated by **Frauke Bahr**

NorthSouth
New York / London

This is Tanya. It's easy to tell when
Tanya doesn't want to do something.

"I WON'T!"

she screams.

What doesn't Tanya want to do?
Sometimes she doesn't want to go shopping.
Or she doesn't want to go home.
Or she doesn't want to wear her warm winter boots
because her sandals are much prettier.

But there is one thing Tanya **REALLY**
doesn't want to do.
Not ever.

"I WON'T comb my hair!"

"I WON'T comb my hair!"

Tanya screams so loudly
that the old man upstairs
and the family downstairs
and the students across the hall
and even people passing by outside
can hear her.
"It's just Tanya," they say,
"the girl who won't comb her hair."

"I WON'T comb my hair!"

"I WON'T comb my hair!"

This has been going on for a long time.
A **very** long time.
Of course her parents often say,
"Tanya, you *must* comb your hair. It's full
of knots and tangles. You're turning into
Tangled Tanya."

And they try to run a comb
through her hair to get rid of
a few of the knots and tangles.

But a few knots and tangles are
not enough. Tanya's hair just gets wilder.
And wilder. And wilder. Until one day
a small bird lands in Tanya's wild, very
tangled hair.

Then a second bird arrives, and they
build a nest together. Soon there are five
small eggs in Tanya's hair. Then the eggs
begin to crack, and five chicks hatch.

The birds are very busy because the chicks
are always hungry, so Tanya helps out the best
she can.

One day, the whole nest, with all five chicks
in it, almost tumbles down when Tanya bends
over to pick up a worm.

From then on, Tanya is very careful. No more playing tag. No more bouncing on the trampoline. That's much too dangerous.

No more swimming either—and Tanya loves to swim.

It's not easy being Tangled Tanya.

One night, Tanya hears some strange sounds. Loud
and wild sounds. Sounds she has never heard before.
The sounds croak and caw. They rumble and growl.
They hiss and spit. And they are all coming from her hair!
Tanya is frightened. What could they be?

1. A purring panther, black as night
2. Hissing snakes—do they bite?
3. Howling monkeys, talking, talking
4. Jungle parrots, screeching, squawking *and*
5. Half a dozen I-don't-know-whats

What's going on in Tanya's crazy hair?
Who is creeping around up there?
"Be careful!" squawk the parrots.
"You're shaking our tree!"

"Grrrrrrrr!"

growls the panther.

This isn't fun anymore!

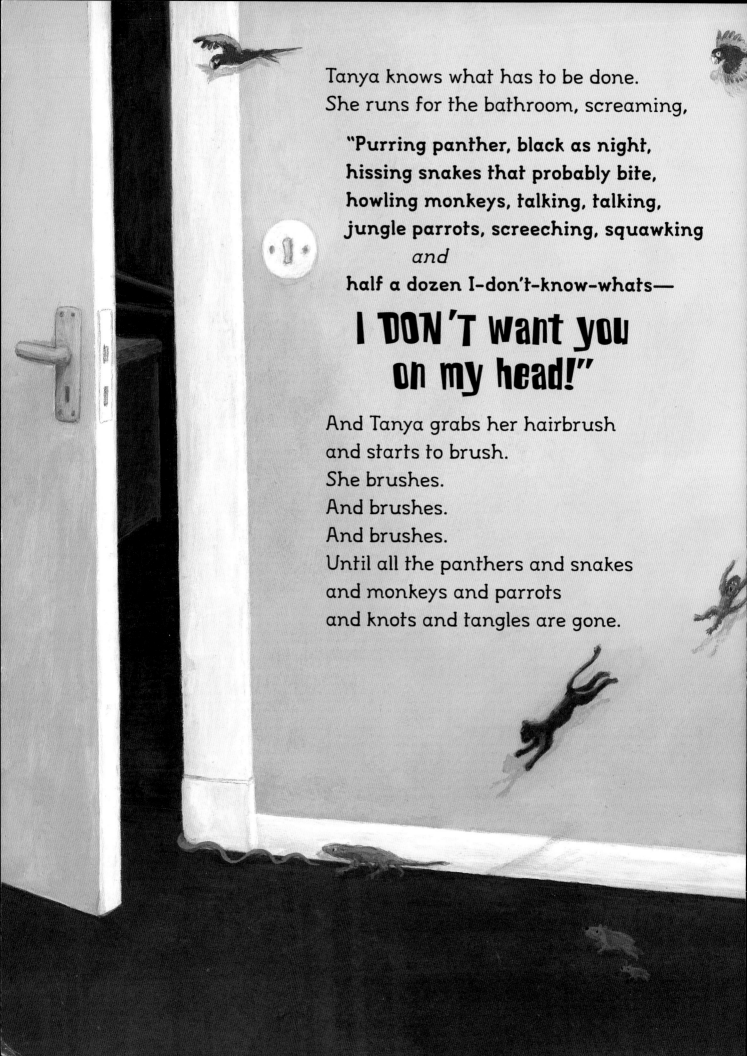

Tanya knows what has to be done.
She runs for the bathroom, screaming,

"Purring panther, black as night,
hissing snakes that probably bite,
howling monkeys, talking, talking,
jungle parrots, screeching, squawking
and
half a dozen I-don't-know-whats—

I DON'T want you on my head!"

And Tanya grabs her hairbrush
and starts to brush.
She brushes.
And brushes.
And brushes.
Until all the panthers and snakes
and monkeys and parrots
and knots and tangles are gone.

Since that day, Tanya combs her hair twice a day.

But if you think she must be quieter now,
you are **wrong!** Every morning, Tanya tries
out so many fantastic hairstyles, she can't
decide which she likes best.

Now every morning
when her parents call,
"Hurry up, Tanya,
it's time to go!"
Tanya shouts back, **"NOT YET!**

I'm still combing my hair!"

She yells so loudly
that the old man upstairs
and the family downstairs
and the students across the hall
and even people passing by outside
can hear her.

They shake their heads and sigh.
"It's just Tanya," they say,
"combing her hair."